The storm on the lost island

Author: Luis Arturo Acevedo Acevedo

Thanks

My fundamental thanks to those who live all the processes of my life, my family: to my wife Eliana, who always understand and patiently respect my immersion for hours between books, leaving other pleasures for later, for example, the Sunday walk or the summer ice cream. To them my infinite thanks for your understanding and support.

To my parents and to our productive talks and useful life advice, where I often took refuge pleasantly.

To my brothers, of whom I have learned a lot, who unwittingly infected me with the passion for writing.

To the work friends who trusted me to carry out the knowledge and translate them into books.

To the acquaintances, to their questions, concerns and demands, that they have taught me so much. To all those entrepreneurs who fundamentally taught me that dreams with action are productive realities.

To my clients, who every day allow me to work in order to elaborate better products.

To all of you who invest their time in reading these ideas, thank you very much for being there, and welcome.

Index

The storm on the lost island

Chapter 1

And I was hundreds of kilometers from the Colombian mainland, I was fishing on the island of Serranilla, a piece of land in a strange way, The area, which was once inhabited, It has houses and some military installations, which were used by US Marines during the Missile Crisis of Cuba in 1962, is now completely uninhabited. The ruins of the buildings in which the old inhabitants of the island lived and worked, give the island a gloomy and grayish air that has caused even the sailors to define it as the ghost island.

Serranilla is a former atoll. It is about 40 km wide and 32 km long, with an area of 1,200 km², almost entirely of water. Several very small keys emerge from the waters to form the islands of the bank; the area began as a small community. The last inhabitants left Serranilla, leaving a place in which only the climate and other natural elements have modified the physiognomy of the island.

Surrounded by huge blocks of reinforced concrete to defend against the waves, the same ones that give it that rare shape, Serranilla came to house many soldiers. By then the insula it had hospitals, several stores and even a small room where the military relaxed after arduous shifts on the high seas.

My name is Anderson; I had the opportunity to enter the prohibited areas of the island. In their images a world is glimpsed in silence, without movement, in which time seems to have stopped forever. This almost inert planet, inheritance of the industrial revolution.

The island, receives every day a few tourists who travel in some of the boats of the various companies that have authorization to enter the area. The visit is limited to a few hours and during the same it is only allowed access to three areas near the old houses and the area of the military that lived in this place.

The small military buildings are the only ones that visitors can contemplate in all their immensity (without being able to enter them). The birds that fly over the area and the buzz of the waves crashing against the gigantic dam that surrounds the island are the most common sounds of this geographical feature that once housed this small community.

The ruins of the central office, with its orange bricks, or the entrance to the second tunnel of the base are other facilities that can still be seen in detail on the island. Due to the isolation of the area, there was a great loss of houses due to its cracking and humidity.

Serranilla, is as impressive as described in some sailors. Recently the insula has returned to attract attention due to its unknown beauty I have impenetrable and - especially for being an uninhabitable area.

The island is today a metaphor for the evolution of some of those tides. Afloat, barely accessible to mortals and with a place that takes your breath away, the island has earned the nickname of the ghost island, a very correct description for those who visit this uninhabited area.

Already back to San Andres islands of Colombia. After an exhausting trip to Serranilla after fishing all day. I decided to go to the bar to take with other fishing friends. The other had a strong drunkenness, sore and battered, his mind numbed by the run of blood and with dry tongue, I opened my eyes to return to life. I did not know where I was or what to expect or why I was floating in that stinking gray limbo that was not in control of my body. However, I soon understood that the pain was due to my being immobilized on the bed. My head was buzzing. On the bed lay the lower half of my body, impeded from all movement by a jumble of sheets while the other half rested on the floor, lovingly hugging a pillow damp with sweat. A nauseating breath reminded me of the causes of that mess: I had caught it well. It can be seen that the intoxication had not given me time to undress because I was without pants, but with my shirt and socks in place.

Through the blinds in my room, an accurate beam of sunlight and the irritating, distant and stubborn sound of a traffic light for the blind. Both phenomena, indifferent to my state, pierced my brain.

Helped by the bedside table that was from before, robust and well built; I managed to sit on the floor. My head, slowly, began to work. While my physical discomfort subsided, the harmful effect of my remorse grew exponentially. I felt irresponsible. I knew that, in that room rented as a writer in disgrace, I was sinking forever. I stood up. In a show of will of those that I use to do what I owe and not what I want, I decided to take a shower, so, as soon as the floor stopped dancing, I got under a jet of cold water and in a few minutes I came back to life.

When I went down to the street it was almost noon. Looking for something for the headache after taking seemed to be the best option to start the day; but the neighborhood the hill, an old sea-faring slum that I frequented when I wanted to get away from the hustle and bustle, attracted me in the opposite direction. Back, dead with laughter, I left my money.

The hill is a penumbrous neighborhood of the marine stroll. It is on a corner with a dirt road and opens directly to the sea. From this they separate a tiled terrace without walls, a wide curb of tiles, a stone parapet and a strip of sand that is lost in both directions. There are many establishments that remain in the neighborhood whose hallmarks sink into the past. From its walls hang nets, gear, stuffed fishes, rigging, a rudder -of the real ones- and an endless supply of junk belonging to the past sailor of Stephen's father, his current owner. The atmosphere of the establishment subjugates and goes back to the times when the quarrels made the work of any storyteller easier.

Predictably, there was no one on the terrace. All the tables were at my disposal and I could choose the best corner to feel sorry for myself. However, Stephen had to ruminate other plans for that day, because he soon appeared with his eternal cloth tied to the waist and two beer mugs. We were old acquaintances. His presence, normally restrained, did not alter my mood, although, on that occasion, I was surprised to get up a chair and sitting next to me.

- What happens? He said with his ineffable weary tone and carefree.

"Nothing," I answered. But the statement was far from certain because, between my eyebrows, I had gotten the idea that some sailor was going to favor with my professional neglect and was going to gain positions in the intricate ocean. I had low self-esteem.

- Have you finished fishing?

-No, I have not even started, but do not worry, something will occur to me, it's a matter of putting up with patience.

"All right," he said, "that reassures me ... Last night I saw you at sea.

-Yeah, I was fine, right?

-Yes, a lot ... You lacked a court to maneuver.

Stephen is a man around sixty-five, stubborn, lonely, patient and, perhaps, too quiet. Is a good person. For my taste, at the time, it was too much materialistic. That was an aspect of his personality that took away points in my esteem and, so much so, that when I saw him sneaking around with his huge book of accounts peeping over his shoulder, like a miser who needed to hide the magnitude of his wealth , me I would take him away from him and cut him off from complicity. His business, although we never talked about it, monopolized all his desires. However, I appreciated it sincerely.

For a long time, Stephen, sitting parallel to me, remained silent. He savored his drink and licked his thick mustache without paying me the slightest attention. I was waiting. I needed someone, a friend, an accomplice, a comrade with a certain sensibility, to listen to my lamentations. Anyone who joined my sorrows, but that person, obviously, was not my dinner companion. Stephen worked on another frequency. His half-closed eyes were walking along the bodies lying in the sand on the beach, stopping, at intervals, at the young women who sunbathed in the sun. Surely he gauged his outdated possibilities for conquest.

"Look at that blonde," she said suddenly, pointing to a beauty. "She is the most exquisite being on earth. I knew some of his old romantic stories, but that comment did not seem appropriate to his discretion.

- Which? The one who comes here?

-The same.

- What's so special about it? Do you know her?

-Yes -was his laconic answer, but he said it with such a face of a decapitated sheep that, forgetting my own troubles, I felt that I was laughing. I could not help but tease him.

- Do not you think you're a little older to make the hummingbird? That dish is no longer for your teeth. - But I kept looking at the girl. In fact, she was a very beautiful tourist who moved insecurely on the hot sand and who, by age, could well have been my daughter in the remote case that some unconscious had proposed it to me. For a moment I forgot my afflictions.

The young girl advanced determined towards us that we saw approaching with dazzled eyes of moth-eaten hulk.

"Hello," the girl said with a beautiful smile as she reached the table.

"Hello," we answered both at once.

- Will you sign an autograph? His sweet, singsong voice was addressed to me, as he handed me a small notebook.

- Who me? "My joy in a well," I thought, "was mistaken as a character."

-Yes, you.

- Are you sure it's my autograph what you want? Do you know who I am?

- Sure, Anderson, a great fisherman, adventurous sometimes and survivor of great marine catastrophes. The tirade ran out of him. Stephen allowed himself the license of a sly smile while I dropped my chin.

-Well, yes, indeed, that's me. -I reacted and, like a good veteran of a thousand battles, I took his notebook and tried to hide my embarrassment with another question-. And what's your name?

-Johana -was the simple answer. "The name," I thought at that moment, "comes close to fitting." He was very young, much more than he had believed when he saw her from a distance before the stone wall jumped. His figure was sharp against the blue of the sea and a huge smile lit his face.

I know that I was not able to be original in the dedication that I wrote in the notebook.

She would be sick of hearing what I put on her green eyes, her blond hair and her incomparable beauty; I cursed myself inside. It bothered me to look like an old green man in front of a young girl.

However, she thanked my attention and remained motionless by the table as if she expected me to add something else. It was Stephen who ventured a way out.

-Hey, why do not you sit down and tell my friend where you know him from? Stephen's intervention was a surprise to me. It is not usually released.

Besides, it never crossed my mind that she could accept such an invitation, but I saw that this was not my best day to reason. Johana, just as subtle as my friend, answered:

-Alright. -And a chair approached.

Chapter 2

So much self-confidence in a person his age intrigued me to the same extent that I was flattered by the fact that he had recognized me. I figured I would not be too busy, but I did not care. It was a beautiful novelty on that ill-fated morning.

As soon as Johana sat down in front of me, Stephen, as if he had been connected to the batteries, stood up and with a malevolent smile of old Celestina asked:

- What do I bring you to drink?

"A beer," she said, still looking at me with a mischievous expression on her face.

- And good? -I said- Where do you know me? It does not seem that you are old enough to be interested in my trips to the sea; they have little interest for young people. -It was my stubborn way to atone for my faults. She did not have compassion.

- Something certain there is in what it says, Mr. Anderson. Before his way of being was fresher than now, more loosely and, although the irony has not changed, the one now seems a bit caustic. It is as if he wanted to punish himself while criticizing others. But I still like it.

-Studies psychology, right? -It was the first thing that occurred to me when listening to his comment. I did not realize that, with that statement, I was just giving him the reason.

-No, but you do not need to notice the changes.

- Since when do you know what I do?

"Since I have use of reason," he answered. Although, in fact, it was my parents who told me and I who listened to the conversations. They started laughing. They said it was sharp and incisive; that did not leave puppet with head. My father, especially, is an unconditional follower. Now, since he divorced my mother, we do not have many occasions to comment on these things because we see little, but in my adolescence we did not do anything else.

- Do you live here, in the neighborhood?

-No, I live with my mother in another neighborhood, on the island of San Andrés, and we come from time to time to this neighborhood.

- How old are you, Johana? -I could not avoid it.

-Nineteen-For some reason, when the girl said age I felt a twinge in her side. It was as if he confirmed my unquestionable old age. He thought it was smaller, right?

"No, on the contrary, I assumed you would have twenty or something else," I lied. But it is also true that I do not usually talk much with young people...

At that moment, from the beach, someone shouted her name, urging her to leave the conversation. Johana, come! Let's go! The girl raised her head and turned to face the sea. A group of young people waved at him.

- They are your friends?

-Yes, they are my gang here, in the neighborhood. I have to go.

-Of course, leave. I loved talking to you, it's a pity that my friend forgot your beer, but it will be again. If you're still here, we'll see you another day.

"Sure, I know where to find him." And with that, with a smile from ear to ear, he stood up and went to the door of the bar to say goodbye to Stephen. You take care of yourself!! - Then he ran to the beach leaving me in one piece.

For some reason, even today, I am unable to imagine Stephen as a member of a family group; with a house, a woman or a daughter like Johana, exchanging opinions at breakfast about my old stories of the sea. His image, always, comes to me associated with the neighborhood the hill (which is still as old and untidy) and the confusion that I felt that midday caressed by a brackish air that ascended from the sea.

Stephen did not return to my table until after a long time. I expected it with the weapons loaded. During the wait I had made a thousand guesses about what would have happened if, in an attack of euphoria, I had insinuated to the daughter or criticized the father or, simply, I would have offended either of them because of my state of mind. All my speculations ended in disaster. He should never have laid that trap for me. However, when my friend emerged from the gloom of the place, again parapet behind a couple of beers, I kept waiting for me to walk to send it to walk. It did not happen. The talk with Johana had restored me a certain amount of confidence in my skills as a conversationalist so that I prepared to speculate with his mistake.

- What? To what was he right? He said after sitting as usual, with his eyes on the horizon...

- Reason? Reason in what?

- In what is the most exquisite being on earth?

He did not smile when he said that. Mentally, I had no choice but to agree with him.

-Hey, Stephen, did I never tell you that you're a scoundrel?

"No," he answered, "but neither is it necessary, I always knew that.

-You never told me you had a daughter.

-You did not ask me either. I have it almost twenty years ago and it is the main cause of my continuing in this hole. The comment had come from the soul.

- You mean the bar? It was very strange that he expressed himself that way. The bar, as far as I knew, represented his whole life.

-I mean the bar, the neighborhood and everything that keeps me anchored in this place. This has been an imposition of Johana's mother; his punishment. But I guess I deserved it. It has taken me many years to realize.

-I had no idea. I have always believed that you were here of your own free will.

-Do not. Of its own accord it would be far away. "Stephen's face was, at that moment, an immutable mask in which the winds and salt of many seas had drawn an indecipherable map. That was the price I had to pay to see Johana grow. Between a judge and my wife they took the sea. In the end, as expected, I got used to staying on land, but he has been a hard friend of mine, very hard. He had once again plunged into a distant silence. However, I was not willing to leave things at that point. Whatever his personal situation was, he did not give me the right to play the trick of letting go of the ring without warning me.

-And, what did you expect me to do when leaving me alone with her? That he will play the riddles? What will the yews do? That has been a trick. You know it, do not you?

- Play game? No man no. I know them both. You can be salty, but you're just a bad apprentice. You have your code and your ethics.

- Any ethics is skipped before such a chocolate - Suddenly I wanted to annoy him the day-. I was about...

-I do not think so, but, having seen the slightest hint of that you say, you would have seen me really angry, I was watching you.

- Oh, you had us under surveillance. I said, Stephen, you're a real scoundrel...

"Besides, she admires you, man." Stephen turned to me for the first time. His eyes, dwarfed by the glare, looked like two burning slits that rummaged in my brain. Think you're a sailor with deep convictions, maybe I told you. See you and follow you as many times as you come to the neighborhood, comment on your adventures. Asks me...

-And you, what do you say? What am I finished? That I am not able to be at sea for a long time and lose on Sunday and that's why I get drunk to have an excuse? What do you tell him? My hands trembled with indignation. Suddenly I was realizing that the opinion of that young girl had become important and I was worried about the image she might have of me. Stephen kept watching me. Surely, he noticed my frustration.

-I do not tell you anything, friend, she draws her own conclusions. Today, I'm sure, he did not take any of those impressions you say. Besides, I'll tell you, he learned to value your work long before you felt like shit. I could not help but remember Johana's words: "My father is an unconditional follower." «They started laughing ...». «They said that they considered it sharp and incisive; that did not leave puppet with head ».

- He told me, yes. He also told me that you are an enthusiast of my work, but now that I know he was referring to you, I do not believe it. And you know what? Nor do I believe that this meeting today was casual. I imagine that all this is the product of a machination of yours to give me a hand because you know I'm finished. I accept that Johana is your daughter, it would be very hard for you to lie to me about that, however, I am sure that she neither knows me nor has ever heard of Anderson Of course, I thank you for the intention, I know what it means to see a friend collapse like a jelly; It is pathetic, but it is the law of life; Some fall so that others can take their place ... - Stephen kept looking at me, surprised by my explosion, without saying a word. Suddenly, as if making an unexpected decision, he pushed aside his chair and stood up. He made a gesture with his mouth that could have been anger and went to his place. I did the only thing that occurred to me at that time: I downed my glass and imitated it, but I left in the opposite direction.

- Hey, come here! -I heard you called me leaning at the door- Do not leave yet; I want to show you something. - Under the arm brought his book of accounts and threw it with fury on the table. It was a heavy volume so that the glasses oscillated and, for a moment, I thought they would go to hell. I retraced my steps.

- What happens? Now are you going to tell me your sorrows?

- Open this wherever you want! You think I do not know what you think. Open it! Maybe there is something that interests you to know. Stephen's face was transformed. I did not want to see it like that, it was painful enough to carry my sorrow to feel, in addition, the weight of my friend's. I opened the book. For a moment I did not understand what I was seeing. A blurred cloud covered my understanding and the lazy gears of my brain seemed to accuse, again, the symptoms that had tormented me all morning. Before my eyes the old book had been transformed into a scrapbook with countless calls to the margin, clarifications, comments...

- What is this? -I managed to articulate.

-This is: almost your whole life. They are your adventures since you entered the sea, the trips you have made, and the ones that listened to you, your criticisms ... Everything. What you see on the sidelines are our comments; mine and those of my ex-wife; there are many of Johana-Stephen was also upset. I wrote them last night, you know, after seeing you drunk, "he said. I did it to coax you; it has nothing to do with my admiration or my respect for your work ... "I did not know what to say.

I simply closed my ears and let it go while the pages of the book went by one by one; a crazy job, a painstaking job that must have taken him a very long time to reconcile.

Finally, Stephen also fell silent and let me go through those pages loaded with history.

"You are crazy, my friend," I murmured without looking at him. "This could only happen to you; a sailor with a lot of patience and a lot of free time ... "When I looked up I noticed the glazed look.

"Do not give up, Anderson," was all he said as we hugged. Do not give them that taste...

Today, as I talk about my adventures, I remember that scene in the bar and I think about my efforts to contain the tears during my return to the floor.

Eager, I look with a look full of gratitude to my old friend Stephen and Johana who wanted to be present at the place.

I do not know if they know it, I suppose so, but it has been my panegyric about friendship that has set my colleagues so high.

The heartfelt apology I wrote in his honor and running, in the short span of an afternoon and an endless night, the day after that dreadful drunkenness and left with the book that his friend lent him.

The next day.

The old sailor Anderson was in his room and glancing at the book decided to read it for a moment before leaving and entering the sea.

The book began with the most impressive story that happened to the old life of sailor and fisherman to old Anderson. And it started like this:

Chapter 3

That morning Anderson went deep into the sea to fulfill his routine, was resting on his boat, just then a powerful storm was developing along the sea, in minutes unleashed waves of great size. The speed of the winds and the size of the waves made Anderson desist from returning to the island of San Andrés. The capricious gravity and the fate that made him protagonist of this story were the culprits of subjecting the sailor to the cruel laws of chance; the immense increase of the waves lashed the small fishing boat, they were so much the blows that suffered that the boat began to be destroyed little by little and only gave him the just time to grab a life preserver and to throw to the sea by the last redoubt of the ship above from the waterline. The soundtrack of the escape alternated the screams and chirps of the structure.

When the cold waters reached the engine, the thermal collapse caused a great explosion that ended up sinking the ship. Anderson's only obsession was to swim centrifugally to avoid the suction of the boat in his death. In his flight Anderson saw his ship for the last time on the other side.

While Anderson, exhausted and away from the turbulences and possibilities of survival, remained clinging to a semi-conscious lifeguard for the effort ... after a few hours, and with calm and twilight backlight, Anderson spotted a few hundred meters one of the dirty rafts of support that your boat had. A last effort that saved his life and took away his conscience took him to the surface of what would be his home in the coming days.

With the first lights and heats of dawn Anderson regained consciousness and awakened to the nightmare of reality. His raft, a ramshackle 3 × 3 meter boat with slats wood on drums, contained a small kit designed for the survival of four people during a couple of days. Under a trapdoor on the raft he found:

- Eight cans of small cookies.

A barrel of water of 30 liters.

Two chocolate bars.

-Some lumps of sugar.

-A few flares, two aluminum bowls and a flashlight.

There were no signs of sails or oars, which caused the constant drift of the ship. Anderson estimated that the supplies were enough for about 20 days, so his mood and hope for rescue were quite optimistic.

Anderson spent days and nights trying to find any sign of life. A ship or an aircraft that rescued him, but his efforts were futile and useless. One night, an airplane crossed the sky, standing out in the starry sky. Anderson fired one of the flares and a bright spot broke the darkness of the sea, but then it fell and vanished. No change of trajectory in the plane. Once again, alone in the dark of the night, Anderson leaned his face against the wooden board and fell asleep.

One evening, after his routine exercises swimming among fish around the raft so as not to lose his form, Anderson sat down to meditate in the boat looking for a saving memory on the horizon. His gaze, lost, returned to his past, his childhood, his family, his paintings, his canvases...

... His thinking was confused with reality when he saw a canvas fly about twenty meters from the ship. It was a shipbuilding cloth. Probably, it should be from your ship that sank. Without blinking, Anderson jumped into the water and swam as fast as possible to 'hunt' the burlap.

Anderson used the cloth to improvise a small tent on the raft to protect himself from the sun that was tearing his skin. But luck was even greater when he discovered tied at one end of the canvas, a long rope of hemp that he used to link himself to the raft on stormy days and avoid its loss in the innumerable falls.

With the end of the provisions, the acumen was accentuated. From several weeks Anderson began to develop the most archaic instinct of man; the one that leads him to perpetuate himself above any custom and doctrine.

He dismantled the lantern, useless and worn, to forge a hook with one of its metal pieces. For two days he was conforming it with his teeth and his shoe-hammer until he found the right shape. Hemp rope made line and the last biscuit reserved as bait for the first catch: A small sardine that served as bait, in turn, to larger catches. With the lids of the biscuit boats he improvised sharp knives with which to gut the fish and take off some of the small mollusks and limpets that adhered to the raft and worked best as bait.

Catches were not constant and depended on streams and schools of fish. One afternoon the raft entered an immense fish bank that caused Anderson to literally fill the boat with catches that were used for the days of most shortages.

He put the fish to dry once clean, separating guts, guts and blood stored in the corners of the raft. Such was the accumulation of captures and viscera that began to have a problem of odor and putrefaction preventing, even, its correct oxygenation. He then committed one of the few mistakes of his journey when, by getting rid of the viscera and blood, he caused the arrival of a legion of sharks that were hovering for several days, shooing off any glimpse of fishing and causing the greatest famine crisis of the event.

The sharks did not leave and Anderson had no way to continue fishing. Hunger led him to the only option that remained: he had to hunt a shark.

To do this he returned to manufacture a new hook, larger and stronger, with one of the nails that joined the wooden slats to its structure. With his shoe-hammer and carafe he molded the vast needle that knotted, again, to his hemp (which he braided to increase its thickness and resistance). The last fish head served him as dead bait to cheat his 'great meal'.

As soon as the bait was deposited, the chosen shark (more than a meter) bit and stirred the bait; Anderson knew that his only option was to raise the shark with a dry pull to finish it off with punches in his 'medium'. At 10 minutes he had the shark's intestines canned, the fins to dry and as a soda he had prepared the blood of the liver.

After the consumption of the initial carafe of water. Anderson automated the collection of water from the rains and storms using the double lining of his jacket with a weight and practicing a hole to redirect the inside of the decanter. Until several weeks the rate of rains due to the season had been sufficient but after a great storm that ended with all the solid and liquid provisions and with half a raft a drought began that triggered the dehydration of Anderson.

Defeated by the storm, he watched as the albatrosses and gulls roamed the area alerted by rot on deck. Anderson collected all kinds of seaweed and marine plants from the bottom of the raft and piled them up like a bird's nest to attract the seagulls while he waited crouched and covered with the remains of the canvas.

When an albatross made his dive into the nest with fish remains, Anderson pounced on the animal and beat him neck and life bites to suck his blood and eat his meat. A few days later the rain returned and Anderson regained his share of fresh water.

During one morning of his several weeks in the Caribbean, Anderson was awakened by a strong marine whistle. He thought he had finished his nightmare after spotting an immense American freighter approaching a few kilometers from his raft. But later Anderson, he realized his luck just before the great ship went on long until it lost itself again on the horizon.

A few days earlier Anderson had been visited by an American air squadron, which spotted him and even threw a marker buoy from the air. A storm paralyzed the possible rescue and dispersed the air patrol.

Anderson counted the days with notches on one side of the raft, and the nights with crosses. Later he used small pieces of string to compute the lunar calendar. Over many days, he noticed that the water was more pale green than usual. Many birds were flying around their boat and a lot of seaweed floated on the surface. All these are signs encouraged their hope of a nearby coast.

On the next morning, he saw a small island on the horizon. He had no strength, so waving his arms in an effort to get close fast. The boat changed direction and went to it.

Upon reaching the islet. I see a small accumulation of water that looked like rain and which somewhat calmed his thirst.

Anderson was able to walk with much trouble. His weight loss during the drift was 10 kilograms and he spent several days recovering on the islet and looking for food.

This islet was a very distant point from any land mass, also a place of inaccessibility. "Well, it is rarely visited by human beings.

How far from the mainland can you navigate?

In fact, the entire region around the islet is well known to sailors, who officially call it "Uninhabited Zone of the Caribbean."

Some of the last things that come to mind that we would not even like to imagine is having to be on a desert island with no one for a long time. Having to be in an isolated place, far from any civilization and without much more than your body and your mind ... should not be too pleasant a sensation. However, there have been cases of people who have had to seek life in deserted islands due to accidents suffered on ships or planes and that have led them to stop at these places.

In addition, we have all seen movies that deal with someone who is shipwrecked on a huge desert island. Well, Anderson after so many days trying to survive in the purest Robinson Crusoe style.

Anderson did not expect that living on an island could be so difficult. Since his water supply lasted only two weeks, he had to build a contraption to store and filter a drop of water per minute. His temporary shelter in the wreckage of the ship was over, and he needed to have something new. He managed to cut down an entire tree with the help of a clam shell, but it took him about 11 weeks to carry it out. I was struggling to stay alive.

Anderson was completely alone on a lost and abandoned island. Finding food was his biggest problem, but he managed to find a total of 8 crabs he tried to hunt. Nevertheless, he did not have any hunting equipment, he tried to make a kind of basket, but he did not succeed. Luckily, a crab was stuck in some bushes between the trees. It took about 15 minutes to kill the animal, and the meat gave it more energy. He thought that the hunting experience was something terrible.

One of the things that Anderson was that he had to work hard to stay physically fit. In fact, he had to do exercise sessions often to avoid stagnation, highlighting push-ups, pull-ups on the branch of a tree and squats with stones on the shoulders. In addition, I also used to run sections of about 300 meters along the beach. However, the most complicated part was the mental agony he had to suffer on the island...

The constant feeling of being alone on a large island and the imminent feeling of not being rescued were devoured from within. He built an SOS help signal about 3 meters long, but he thought it would never be visible from the sky. He managed to clear a large area of land and made it even larger. He hoped that if a plane passed by, the pilot could see the help signal and rescue him.

It's the kind of things you see in movies. But, in real life, it is difficult to accept the idea of a single person stranded at sea for days, weeks, and even months, and live to tell the tale.

However, miracles do happen, and not only in Hollywood.

We are not talking about people who float aimlessly or get stuck after they run out of gas or are affected by strong winds only to be picked up by the US Coast Guard a few hours later. Far less common are cases in which individuals are lost at sea long enough to run out of food or drinkable water on board, if they were carrying it. To survive, they can not count on technology or the proximity of a nearby city, town or boat, but must rely on ingenuity, inventiveness and luck. It is difficult to determine how many of these types of stories have a sad ending, in which a sailor dies in the sea, except that it is a much higher number than those who are rescued at the end.

Such happy endings do occur ... given what the rescue agencies have reported and confirmed their versions.

Anderson gained time by rationing the water, and then collected fresh water in an improvised natural vessel. And as for food, I used clothes to catch and collect fish. And he managed to have a makeshift hiding place.

The days, weeks and months were mixed after that. Anderson drank rainwater and ate sea turtles.

I thought 'I'm going to get out of this,' "he said." Go out, go out, go out. "

Chapter 4

Have you thought about survival on an island if we have a shipwreck? We believe that these things do not continue to happen, but we are very wrong. We talk about shipwrecks and get trapped on a desert island. Anderson did not lose hope because he had formed the word "Help" in the sand with palm trees. They had been on the island for many days. A great wave made his Vessel overturned, forcing him to reach this island. This remote island is one of many that exist in our oceans, and it is difficult to have them all located if we are trapped in one. In this case, Anderson's fate will be put to the test quickly. If something like this happens to us, what can we do to survive?

There are several things Anderson did on the island in the middle of the sea. At first, many may think that ending up on a desert island can be like a vacation, with beaches, palm trees, sun, clear and blue waters, etc. However, it is not exactly a place where there are umbrellas to protect from the sun. No loungers on the beach with waiters bringing us a cold beer. And of course there are no hotels to return in the afternoon to shower and have a good dinner. We would soon realize that this paradisiacal island is really a horrible nightmare.

The two ways to end up as the only inhabitants in one of these islands are by a shipwreck by sea or by an air accident. Being stuck in a place like this can in principle give us a panic attack, but the chances of survival are high if certain procedures are followed and the perspective is maintained. Being stuck on an island has its own challenges, but being by the sea, in a warm environment and having some food supply is better than many other situations. It is definitely better than being in a cold place with very low temperatures for example.

To begin with, Anderson remembered that if you are in a situation of survival, you have to have a positive attitude. This can be the difference between life and death. We have many examples where people without a previous experience of survival, have managed to get ahead in long periods before being rescued. Knowing how to adapt to the situation, be calm and think clearly is fundamental in the first days. A negative attitude only leads to despair and enter a cycle of destruction that prevents us from doing what is necessary to survive.

Once Anderson got rid of the initial danger of the accident that had brought him to the island, it is important that he was not injured. He was also alert to avoid causing a wound by being in such a lonely place. It does not matter that the wound is small, since what we are least interested in is having an infection that could put us in a complicated situation. There are no doctors on the island and you may not have had time to take medicines. Avoiding infections is a priority.

Anderson kept the remains of the raft everything that could be useful. Most people think that the first thing to take is water or something to light a fire. Although it is important, the first thing to look for is proper footwear to walk the reefs and the maritime soil (and not step on any poisonous fish). Once he had that makeshift shoe, he could start looking for useful things. On the other hand, they were like typical waterproof boots used by fishermen and sailors, who then served to store water or other things.

The remains of the raft were in themselves a good source to get many things that helped him to survive on the island. There are many things that adapted to your needs. Anderson thought that they could make bunks, shelters, clothes, shoes and many other things. It also depends on the creativity we have, but in an extreme situation we usually have better ideas to use all kinds of objects. Put another way, you can make tools from almost anything.

Anderson's next step was to find a source of water. After a few days without water we will die. Apart from this, if the weather is very hot, in a short time we will have difficulties to think and operate normally if we do not drink water. Most of the islands

They have some source of water, especially if there is a lot of vegetation. If it is one of those rocky islands or that only have sand, then it would have a problem no matter how positive we are. Even so, in this case we have the possibility of using sea water as a resource.

Of course, I knew that you can not drink seawater because I could kill it, but with a few pieces recovered from the raft, I could make a sunscreen by making a simple hole in the ground. It is a very useful way to distill salt water. In the caves there are usually also streams of water that could be used.

Storms were also something that could come in handy, since they could provide a good amount of water. This is why Anderson saw fit to always have objects to keep all the water that falls.

Anderson thought of a place to shelter from the cold and heat and that was crucial. A desert island can go through different temperatures both day and night. Therefore, sunstroke and hypothermia are something that should be taken seriously. It usually occurs on islands where it is very hot during the day; the water condensed in the clouds drops as it evaporates. This water falls frozen, so it is not a good idea to be outside.

He saw it important not to sleep directly on the ground since in this type of islands there are usually snakes, spiders and scorpions that are poisonous. It's not like they can kill us with a bite, but we can have a hard time. The best thing is to do a cleaning of the area where I was going to sleep and make a bonfire in the center. This would make many of these little creatures do not even come near. Snakes are usually very elusive, so they do not usually represent a problem. Even so, you always have to take precautions.

The shelter he built reduced as much as possible the bites of other types of insects. I thought it was a good idea to use the materials that can be found to make a mosquito net. Any cloth could be used to make this net that prevents mosquitoes from biting it at night. He also thought to build the refuge away from the coconut trees, since they usually fall without warning and could give him a good blow.

On the desert island, there was more or less food. Anyway, practically in any island we will always find some kind of mollusk, seaweed and fish. Anyway, Anderson was careful not to poison himself. Intoxication may be more common than you imagine, so extreme caution is necessary. If mollusks are difficult to open, they are generally good to eat. If they open easily, better not eat it. Whenever possible, we must cook what we are going to eat.

When Anderson decided to go fishing, he could do it with any kind of wire and give it a hook shape. The same earthworms that I could find on earth can be used as bait. Fishing to eat is a good way to get by if you were trapped on an island, and the tides could help. On the beach natural pools are formed when the tide comes down, and fish used to be caught. Anyway, you always have to make sure you do not eat something poisonous. A good system to know is to scrub the fish in the hand and see if it produces any reaction. Even so, if there is no reaction you should pass lightly on the lip and wait for another reaction. If nothing happens, it will surely be edible.

Of course, I also had the possibility of fruits and vegetables. Anderson researched the island a bit to see where the best sources of natural food are. If there is any fruit that I did not know, I was careful as it can be poisonous. All this is important if we want survival on an island to be a reality.

Of course, Anderson created a huge message on the beach with everything he had on hand for help. From the air they will be able to see it and the rescue will begin. Anyway, he hoped that everything he knew about survival would help him spend whole days to survive on a desert island.

Even so, even the most resilient fishermen would not have stood the test by the Anderson passed after leaving alone.

This island lost in the sea that nobody has managed to explore many years

The island, within the Caribbean Sea, is one of the few redoubts completely separated from human civilization. A fascinating place that in ancient times was populated by natives so aggressive and hostile that the world simply stopped caring.

Primitives, a group of between 40 and 500 people (never been able to be accurately determined) were part of the so-called isolated villages so remote populations or so lost that once were separated from the rest of civilization.

Most times that isolation was due to geographical or political issues. Others, as this population had fiercely defended any contact with the outside world. Ships, cargo ships, or firearms: the response of the primitives had always been accompanied by indifference and arrows, stones and insults.

Thus, for thousands of years and until an explorer was able to set foot on the island for the first time, they had remained isolated and isolated from the rest of the world. Only one great storm that had hit this small island destroyed all that remained of the population until no survivors were left.

The islet, has a privileged position within the Caribbean Sea, sufficiently isolated from the continent so that a trip there is a good stretch by boat or plane, but also too far from other islets, especially a set of relatively civilized islands and administered by your government but very distant.

This islet was used as a place of exile for prisoners when the Caribbean was a colony of the Spanish Empire; there they were assigned to mining, logging and exploration of natural resources. Some of those prisoners, and the stories around them, ended up being part of the legends around this islet.

The islet itself is much smaller, about 72 square kilometers, roughly the size of the island of Manhattan, in New York. It is surrounded by a thin line of beach, which is the maximum that civilization has managed to discern on the island beyond satellite photos and, above all, a barrier reef. It is too small for settlers or to be of interest to government powers (especially because they are many hours by ship: they are older and have better resources). This underwater coral reef prevents not only large vessels from approaching the island too much, but also leaving it practically inaccessible for 10 of the 12 months of the year. There are many reasons, as detailed some paragraphs below, that have kept the islet isolated from the rest of the world for thousands of years, but the coral reef has been its main natural barrier all that time.

It was appreciated that the contour of firm ground remains invariable, but the reef goes from being submerged to fully expose.

Earthquakes have hit the island with violence. The tectonic plate on which it is located slightly tilted, raising its altitude by 2 meters and causing much of that reef to rise above sea level, further accentuating the barrier between the outside world and the intricate jungle that covers the practically the whole island.

The waters surrounding the island, due to all these factors, have abundant fishing, a fact that has also contributed to the particular history of the place.

The story of how civilization, after centuries of forgetting, recalled the islets and their island begin in the middle of a storm in past centuries

That history goes back until a night in which a ship, coming from the Caribbean, accidentally runs aground. The next morning, in broad daylight, the crew quickly checks two things: on the one hand that a coral reef not registered in the navigation charts of the time is responsible for their misfortune, on the other hand, only about 10 miles away is an apparently desert paradise island. There are no roads or signs of human activity, nor buildings or concrete records on the ship about what exactly they have in front of an islet. The captain, as a precaution, orders everyone to remain on board.

A few days later the crew again warns that several human forms have appeared on the beach. Initially it is thought that they are part of the rescue team that had requested by radio from the moment of the grounding, but a simple pass with binoculars quickly discards this theory: the dark forms belong to natives of very dark skin, totally naked, who scream in his address with a face of few friends and threaten them with stones, bows and other weapons. Nervous in the face of a possible attack, the captain redoubled his request for help by radio.

A few days later, the primitives have even begun to build boats on the beach with the intention of boarding the freighter until; finally, a helicopter approaches to evacuate the crew. The remains of the ship can still be seen from the sky, stranded in the coral.

What the ship's crew did not know is that about 7 years before, an expedition attempted to dock on the island was thwarted by a single warrior who, armed with a bow, began firing with the small boat that approached the beach. One of the arrows managed to hit the thigh of one of the sailors, recording the encounter before which they automatically turned around, got on the boat and quickly forgot the subject, leaving the primitives and their island relatively quiet for a few more years.

As far as we know, the greatest approach on the part of civilization was that some anthropologists managed to exchange gifts (especially coconuts and bananas) with the tribe, but most encounters were tense, rough and, once the presents were accepted, the primitives left very clear with bows and arrows that preferred to be alone. If the welcoming committee was too abundant, they retreated directly and disappeared into the depths of the brush.

This means that we really know very little about their origin, their culture and what life was like inside the islet. Several anthropological studies estimated that they had lived there for 65,000 years and that they are descendants of the first inhabitants of the Caribbean, a fascinating fact. 65,000 years, in perspective, implies that they were there 35,000 years before the last ice age, 55,000 before the last mammoths disappeared and about 62,000 before the Egyptians built the pyramids of Giza.

It had been observed that the turtles had learned to avoid the primitives, since in spite of their beauty the turtles are not the intellectually brightest animals on the planet, the answer is probably due to an evolutionary progression, which points to the permanence during thousands of years of the primitives in those lands. They were naked, but their body ornaments and paintings were very similar to those of other races, with which they probably once shared more than aggression.

That dark skin not only related them to the first Caribbean tribes but also, curiously, has allowed to give rise to some of the theories about the brutal hostility that the primitives showed to any foreigner. It is possible that for years several slave trapping routes stopped in their waters with the intention of capturing natives. The knowledge itself of the island goes back almost 2000 years ago when reference is made to an "island of cannibals" in the middle of the Caribbean. The tribes would be described as "savage and ruthless, they would not hesitate a moment to capture the unwary foreigner and eat it alive."

There are not many references throughout history about the islet and they are still quite ambiguous. Exploration. To get to stand on the islet was used a technique that Spanish settlers had developed in those years: capture a member of a nearby tribe, convince him of their good intentions based on gifts and entertainment, then mount it on a boat and use it as proof of good faith before the natives. It seems that it was possible to find a member of the tribe (something that would prove in a certain sense that at that time the tribe was not so closed).

What is surprising is that other people managed to set foot on the island not once but twice. Time after the first attempt and after knowing that there was a volcano on the island.

The reasons why the island remains isolated from civilization are simple: it does not interest anyone too much. It is not rich in resources, it does not have a particularly strategic position, and the coral reef ensures that access is very difficult during most of the year. On the other hand, the fierceness with which the volcano defends its territory makes it simpler, despite curiosity, simply to ignore it. The question is how much longer that will remain that way.

Meanwhile, the small islet remained a temporary capsule isolated from everything, a primordial and mysterious place away from the claw often more abusive than permissive of man, one of the most fascinating places on Earth.

Anderson was thinking about how lucky he were that there were no more inhabitants on the island, since that very fact would have been enough to survive on this distant island. Those indigenous pasts with a history of savages, hostiles and cannibals would not have allowed him to be a single day alive on the islet.

One day, Anderson was surprised to hear the sound of an airplane passing over him. He gestured to the plane and it dropped some supplies. He got food, water, a radio and a medical kit. When he used the radio to talk to the pilot, it was the first contact he had had with anyone in the many weeks. After a long conversation, he asked the pilot how they were able to find him. The answer was totally impressive: the message written on the beach was seen from far away by the plane. An incredible rescue mission that was made possible thanks to this message.

Anderson returned to life, and with the desire to tell his friends and family the story of his life and survival, a story that few can tell. Leave alive a lonely island of the Caribbean. The island of death.

www.ingramcontent.com/pod-product-compliance
Ingram Content Group UK Ltd.
Pitfield, Milton Keynes, MK11 3LW, UK
UKHW020230250726
13967UKWH00001B/292